3 4143 10000 0075

D1150963

hound

Tanya Landman is the author of many books for children, including *Waking Merlin* and *Merlin's Apprentice*, *The World's Bellybutton* and *The Kraken Snores*, and three stories featuring the characters Flotsam and Jetsam. Of *Blood Hound*, the ninth title in her popular murder mystery series, Tanya says, "When someone suggested banning dogs from my local park, a furious argument broke out – with Dog Lovers on one side and Dog Haters on the other. I wondered what would happen if things turned nasty…"

Tanya is also the author of two novels for teenagers: *Apache*, which was shortlisted for the Carnegie Medal and the Booktrust Teenage Fiction Prize, and *The Goldsmith's Daughter*, which was nominated for the Guardian Children's Fiction Prize. Since 1992, Tanya has also been part of Storybox Theatre. She lives with her family in Devon.

You can find out more about Tanya Landman and her books by visiting her website at
www.tanyalandman.com

Poppy Fields is on the case!

Mondays are Murder
Dead Funny
Dying to be Famous
The Head is Dead
The Scent of Blood
Certain Death
Poison Pen
Love Him to Death
Blood Hound

Also by Tanya Landman

Waking Merlin
Merlin's Apprentice
The World's Bellybutton
The Kraken Snores

For younger readers

Flotsam and Jetsam
Flotsam and Jetsam and the Stormy Surprise
Flotsam and Jetsam and the Grooof
Mary's Penny

For older readers

Apache
The Goldsmith's Daughter

blood
hound

tanya landman

WARRINGTON BOROUGH COUNCIL	
34143100908878	
Bertrams	13/12/2011
JF	£4.99
STO	

This is a work of fiction. Names, characters, places and incidents are either the product of the author's imagination or, if real, are used fictitiously. All statements, activities, stunts, descriptions, information and material of any other kind contained herein are included for entertainment purposes only and should not be relied on for accuracy or replicated, as they may result in injury.

First published 2011 by Walker Books Ltd
87 Vauxhall Walk, London SE11 5HJ

2 4 6 8 10 9 7 5 3 1

© 2011 Tanya Landman

The right of Tanya Landman to be identified as author of this work has been asserted by her in accordance with the Copyright, Designs and Patents Act 1988

This book has been typeset in Slimbach

Printed and bound in Great Britain by Clays Ltd, St Ives plc

All rights reserved. No part of this book may be reproduced, transmitted or stored in an information retrieval system in any form or by any means, graphic, electronic or mechanical, including photocopying, taping and recording, without prior written permission from the publisher.

British Library Cataloguing in Publication Data:
a catalogue record for this book is available from the British Library

ISBN 978-1-4063-2897-4

www.walker.co.uk

For Fred, the original King
of Charisma, and (of course)
Hobson and Sally

Kathleen O'Flannery *switched on the TV and perched nervously on the edge of the sofa. It was her husband, Dermot's, first live broadcast and she desperately hoped it would all run smoothly.*

Things hadn't been easy at home lately, but all that would change now. She could go part-time at work; get the dog she'd always longed for; maybe they could even try for a baby!

Kathleen shivered with apprehension as the title sequence began. She hoped Dermot felt calmer than she did. Her heart was in her mouth and she thought she might actually be sick with fright.

Then suddenly there he was: his handsome face filling the screen, looking cool, calm and collected, reading the local news headlines as if he'd been doing it for years. Kathleen felt a surge of possessive pride.

A second later, the crash of breaking glass diverted her attention. Someone had hurled something at the back door! Vandals, probably: kids chucking dustbins around as usual. She'd better sweep up the glass. If she did it quickly she could be back in time to watch Dermot's next link. But halfway to the kitchen, Kathleen froze. It wasn't vandals. It wasn't kids mucking about.

It was a burglar. In the room. Here. With her. A

masked thief swinging an iron crowbar. Before she had time to scream, Kathleen O'Flannery's plans for a rosy future were shattered.

Swiftly, the intruder searched the house for valuables, running from the crime scene just as the news drew to a close.

"That's all for now, folks." Dermot O'Flannery looked into the camera and winked: that would be his trademark, he'd decided – the quirk that viewers would come to know and love. "Thank you and good night," he added, wondering if his wife was watching.

Kathleen was indeed staring at the screen. But her unblinking eyes would never focus on her husband's face again. By the time the credits rolled, Dermot O'Flannery had become a widower.

a different
planet

My name is Poppy Fields. I'm not a big fan of science fiction, to be honest. Time travel, wormholes, pan-dimensional beings? None of that stuff appeals to me. But during the last summer holidays I had the distinct feeling that Graham and I really had slipped into a parallel universe. Not literally, of course. We hadn't been abducted by aliens or anything. It was way weirder than that.

We'd landed on Planet Dog.

The break had only just begun, but Back to School window displays were already breeding in the shops like gerbils. Every time I went into town I got a horrible prickle of unease. The new school year was looming on the horizon like a mountain that had to be climbed. I did my best to ignore it: I was determined to have a long, lazy summer. My mum, Lili, is a gardener, so she was busy mowing people's lawns and weeding their flower-beds. In theory this left me free to do whatever I liked – i.e. not very much at all. We were in the middle of a heatwave and I was planning to sleep late, eat ice cream and vegetate on a lounger in the garden. I reckoned the toughest decision I would have to make all summer would be whether to lie in the sun or sit in the shade. But it turned out that fate had other plans.

It was all Mrs Biggs's fault. She's our Not Very Observant next-door neighbour. When Mum's working she sometimes asks Mrs B to keep an eye on me. This is less of a problem than you might think: the woman spends all her time watching daytime TV. She'll occasionally bang on the wall during an advert break, and I'll bang back to reassure her I'm still alive, but that's as far as it goes. And if she's watching a film or one of her favourite soaps, she won't even do that. However, this particular August, Mrs Biggs chose to trip over and break her leg. Mum and I were having a barbecue at the time, so we heard the muffled thud followed by the horrible groan and the indignant yapping. Never slow to respond to a drama, we rushed round immediately and Mum administered first aid while I called an ambulance. The paramedics arrived in a wail of sirens, and before long Mrs Biggs had been carted off to be X-rayed and encased in plaster.

We were left with Bertie.

Bertie was None Too Pleased about his owner's apparent abduction. He sat on the doormat and stared at Mum and me as if assessing our weak points and considering How Best to Attack. He wasn't a big dog, but he still managed to look fairly threatening.

"I told her we'd look after him," said Mum nervously.

"Did you?"

"Yes … just while she's laid up. You won't mind walking him, will you? It's the holidays, after all. It's not like it will interfere with your school work. We owe it to her really, after all the times she's looked after you…"

So that was it. I was officially volunteered as Bertie's Exercise Supervisor; his Personal Trainer; his Attendant and Servant. I had to walk him twice a day, armed with a pooper-scooper and antibacterial poop bags. (Let me say right here and now that until you've dealt with a bag of warm dog poo you don't know the meaning of the word "gross".)

Maybe, if Mrs Biggs had possessed a cooler animal, I wouldn't have minded quite so much. An Alsatian, say, or a Rottweiler. A bull terrier, even. Something slightly menacing; something with a bit of street cred. But no. Bertie is a Pekinese.

If you've never encountered one of these before, let me explain. He's got bulgy eyes that look as if they might pop clean out of his head if you squeeze him in the wrong place. His nose is squashed up like he's been rammed into a brick wall, and his legs are so short they're entirely concealed by a vast amount of fur. Frankly, he looks more like a hairy maggot than a mammal. Cute, I suppose, if you like that kind of thing. I can't say I did, at least not to begin with.

You might think that his size and general lack of awesomeness would give him an inferiority complex, but as far as Bertie's concerned, he's the King of Charisma. Which is just as well, because before the summer was out Bertie's Impressively Large Ego had literally saved my life.

The morning after Mrs Biggs's accident, Graham and I reported for Walking Duty. I'd roped Graham in to help because I didn't have a whole lot of experience in the dog-handling department and felt in need of moral support. Graham wasn't a dog expert either, but, being Graham, he'd done his background research. He'd gone straight to the local library after I'd phoned him and borrowed armfuls of books on the subject. By the time we arrived on Mrs Biggs's doorstep the following morning, his knowledge of Canine Management, Dog Breeds and Training Techniques was second-to-none.

We rang the doorbell to let Mrs Biggs know we'd arrived but then used the spare key to let ourselves in. As Mrs Biggs was encased in plaster from thigh to toe, she couldn't get off the sofa without a monumental amount of effort. Bertie clearly thought I was Personally Responsible and glared at me accusingly the second I stepped into the lounge.

"Now, dear," said Mrs Biggs, "Bertie's all ready to go. Looking forward to a nice walk, aren't you, Bertie? Oh, and you'll need to pop into the vet's on the way back. Bertie's out of his eye-drops. I've phoned to let them know you're coming." She handed me some cash from her purse and then picked up Bertie's lead.

Thinking *she* was taking him for a walk, Bertie was ecstatic, chasing his tail in circles and huffing like an excited piglet. When Mrs Biggs handed the lead to *me*, however, his expression changed to one of Extreme Resentment. He sat down, leant hard against Mrs Biggs's plastered leg and point-blank refused to move.

Graham, armed with inside information, took over. He clicked his tongue and said, "Walkies!" with all the authority he could muster.

Bertie gave him the dirtiest of disgustingly filthy looks and refused to budge.

"Oh dear," said Mrs Biggs fretfully. "Now don't be difficult, Bertie. You need your exercise." She smiled encouragingly at us. "You'll just have to carry him a little way. As soon as he knows you're taking him to the park he'll be fine."

She was lying.

Graham carried Bertie along the road while Mrs Biggs watched from her front room. As soon as we turned the corner he put the dog down. Bertie sank onto the pavement like a deflated beach-ball. He wouldn't move a millimetre.

"I thought dogs were supposed to like walks," I said crossly.

"Yes, I rather had that impression too. I suppose he hasn't read the *Complete Dog Maintenance Manual*." Graham gave me one of his blink-and-you-miss-it grins.

The only way to get Bertie to the park was to carry him the entire way. We took it in turns after discovering that, for a small animal, he was surprisingly heavy. I half suspected he was putting on weight as we walked. When we finally got to the park gates we set him on his feet again, and to our immense relief he trundled off happily enough. We were a bit reluctant to let him off his lead in case he made a bolt for home, so we sort of trailed along behind him. To be honest, now *he* was taking *us* for a walk.

Bertie isn't what you might call the athletic type. He bumbled along, stopping to pull up a weed here or prune a twig there, which he then held gripped between his lips like a gangster's cigarette stub. Every time we encountered daisies he carefully bit their heads off. As we ambled behind the Incredible Gardening Pekinese, Graham and I found ourselves entering a parallel universe: Planet Dog.

Graham and I had both been to the park hundreds of times before, but it was only when we were there with Bertie that I discovered the strange and interesting fact that dog owners inhabit a whole different world. I'm fascinated by human behaviour and I'd noticed before that the people who visit the park can generally be split into distinct groups. You've got the mothers with small kids who hang around the playground during the day, and when they go home for tea, the same area becomes taken over by gangs of teenagers. There's the football crowd who play matches at weekends, and the old folk who gather around the bowling green and the café. And then there are the dog walkers. The people in the other groups are all locked up in their own worlds and don't chat to anyone else. But the dog walkers have clearly never been told: "Don't talk to strangers".

We hadn't been there more than ten minutes before we'd met at least a dozen new people and their dogs. While the dogs sniffed noses (and various other parts of each other), their owners made polite conversation with us. They all knew Bertie – he was like a Canine Celebrity – and did double takes when they saw us escorting him and not Mrs Biggs. We had to explain about her broken leg over and over again.

The first dog we met was Jessie, a shaggy, yellow animal that was so big and bouncy she almost knocked me off my feet. ("A fine example of a golden retriever," Graham assured me.) The young man walking her – or more accurately racing/romping/playing/rolling-about-in-the-grass with her – had similarly shaggy, yellow hair. He looked like he ought to be surfing off a sandy beach somewhere in Hawaii or Australia.

The next dog we encountered was Sam, who gave Bertie only the most cursory of sniffs before turning his attention back to the ball that his owner – a wiry, athletic woman – was throwing for him. ("A Border collie. They're excellent for obedience work," Graham told me, "but they need an awful lot of exercise.") Then we came across a small Spanish woman with a large Great Dane named Hamlet, followed by Gertrude, a long, thin dachshund who was accompanied by a short, fat man. When we turned the corner we found a confused elderly gentleman standing in the shrubbery. He was smartly dressed (despite the heat) in a flat cap, tweed jacket and bow tie, and was carrying a collar and lead but had no other evidence of dog ownership (i.e. no visible dog). "Have you seen Byron?" he asked anxiously. "My beagle's picked up a scent. Lord alone knows where he's got to now!"

"Erm … no," I replied. Without another word the man disappeared into the bushes in search of the runaway.

"What's a beagle?" I asked Graham.

"Hound," he said, as if that explained everything. "Originally bred for hunting rabbits," he added. "From what I've read, he hasn't got a hope of calling him back if the dog has smelt something interesting."

Last, but definitely not least, we encountered Malcolm and Stanley, two exceedingly round and fluffy creamy-white dogs about the same size as Bertie. "Shit Sue," Graham muttered under his breath.

Or that's what I thought he said. "What?" I asked, astonished. Making rude personal remarks isn't like Graham at all.

He looked at me narrowly and then said carefully, "Shit. Sue. Two separate words. Spelt S–H–I–H T–Z–U. They're a very popular breed of dog."

"Oh," I said. "Right."

Malcolm and Stanley appeared to be on friendly terms with Bertie. They all wagged tails and sniffed bottoms while Malcolm and Stanley's large, rosy-cheeked owner made sympathetic noises about Mrs Biggs's leg and hunted for her bag of doggy treats. When they were done sniffing and licking and exchanging other peculiar canine greetings (I didn't like to watch too closely), the three dogs sat down and looked at the woman expectantly. This was clearly part of their daily ritual.

Malcolm and Stanley's owner was the kind of person who speaks to dogs as if they're exceedingly dim, slightly deaf, very small children. "Sweetie time," she trilled. "Look what Mumsiewumsie's got for you. Now then, boys, who's going to be first? Who is? Who is? Who's going to be first?"

Graham and I had to avoid each other's eyes so we wouldn't get the giggles, but I have to confess I took a certain pride in the way Bertie behaved. He wasn't going to miss out on a treat, but he wasn't going to compromise his dignity either. He didn't wag his tail. He just sat and waited, and I swear that under all that hair he had one eyebrow raised. Malcolm and Stanley, on the other hand, were downright silly. They yapped and wagged and spun around in circles. Then Malcolm leapt for the proffered treat like an enthusiastic dolphin.

"Naughty boy," said Mumsiewumsie sternly, wagging

her finger at him. "Now if you can't behave, Malcolm, you won't be getting no sweeties, will you? I've told you over and over again, you've got to be nice." She turned to her other dog. "You show him how it's done, Stanley. You've got to be polite, haven't you? Naughty boys don't get no sweeties, do they?"

Well, Stanley didn't perform much better than Malcolm, and after seeing the way he snatched his treat, I was kind of surprised that Mumsiewumsie had managed to retain all her fingers for so long. When she came to Bertie, he took his treat perfectly politely and then turned his back on her. Bertie didn't do waggy-tailed enthusiasm and he didn't do gratitude, either.

One dog owner who didn't stop to talk to us was a young woman with amazing auburn hair, who sprinted past so quickly she almost mowed Bertie down. I felt quite indignant on his behalf but there was no point protesting: her headphones were rammed so far into her ears she wouldn't have heard a thing. Plus she had a very big dog – whose coat was the same colour as her hair – literally running rings around her. Get in his way and you were likely to be flattened.

"Irish setter," said Graham. "Commonly known as a red setter, for obvious reasons."

We were watching the super-speedy runner and her dog disappear into the middle distance and didn't notice the approaching toddler. Bertie had vanished into the undergrowth to do some more pruning. Graham and I had stopped, waiting patiently on the end of the extending lead for him to re-emerge into the sunshine.

Meanwhile, the toddler – a boy of what, two, three years old? – was pottering towards us. His mother was a couple of metres behind him, pushing another baby in a twin buggy.

The parks department had been out watering the flower-beds that day, and some of the water had run off and pooled in a dip at the edge of the path. The boy splashed happily into it and sat down.

He looked so funny sitting fully clothed in the middle of a puddle that his mum laughed and so did we, and everything was fine until Bertie decided to join in. He trotted out from under a bush, waded across the puddle and flopped down right next to the boy.

Now I'm not what you might call a dog enthusiast, and I have to admit that they sometimes frighten me. But at that moment Bertie looked like the least scary canine in the entire universe: there was absolutely nothing even remotely worrying, aggressive or terrifying about that big ball of fluff on very short legs.

And yet that little boy screamed. Screamed and screamed and screamed as if Bertie was about to tear him to pieces.

The small boy wasn't the only one who had what Graham later described as "a somewhat disproportionate reaction to Bertie's behaviour". His previously happy, smiling mother swooped across the path, plucked her son from the water and then – to my utter horror – gave Bertie the kind of kick you usually only see in rugby internationals. The poor dog flew through the air and was only saved from a nasty injury by Graham catching him.

"You should keep that thing under control," the woman yelled at us, "and not let it go around scaring kids! I've a good mind to call the police and report it as a dangerous dog. It would be destroyed, you know!"

Graham and I looked at Bertie. No, he hadn't suddenly morphed into a killer wolfhound. Our mouths opened and closed but nothing useful fell out. Her attack was so completely unexpected and so utterly undeserved that neither of us could think of anything to say. Cuddled up in Graham's arms, Bertie looked the picture of wounded innocence. I wanted to cover his ears so he couldn't hear the death threats.

What with her yelling and the boy screaming and the baby in the pushchair bawling there was quite a commotion going on, and everybody in the park seemed to be staring at us. Things only got worse when the next dog walker rounded the corner.

While Bertie was the least fearsome thing on four legs imaginable, this next dog was exactly the opposite.

"Mastiff," said Graham automatically. "An attack dog. Used by the Spanish to conquer the Aztec Empire."

"Oh?" I said. "How?"

Graham clutched Bertie a little more tightly, although whether that was for Bertie's protection or his own was hard to say. "They tore the Aztecs' throats out."

I gulped nervously. But if Graham and I were alarmed at the sight of the slobbering animal dragging its owner towards us on a length of chain, the woman and her children were terrified. The toddler was so scared he stopped screaming. The baby stopped bawling. They both fell into a frozen silence while their mother went a ghastly shade of green, swaying slightly as if she might faint. She then rallied enough to swing the pushchair round so that both children were behind her, and she raised her hands, clenching them into fists as if preparing to defend her offspring to the death.

The young man on the end of the chain – close-cropped hair, black hoodie emblazoned with skull motifs – knew full well the effect his dog was having. A thoughtful owner might have changed direction, or at least given the kids as wide a berth as possible. But this guy wasn't the thoughtful type. "Come on, Tyson," he growled and walked past us, keeping so close that

I could feel the dog's hot breath on my bare legs. It paused to stare at Bertie and I could almost see a doggy thought bubble pop out of its head – "What the hell is *that*?" I thought we were done for, but luckily the creature shook its head in disbelief, spattering me with flecks of drool from the knee down, and then carried on with its walk. I didn't complain about the spittle. The owner wasn't the kind of person you made complaints to, not if you wanted to live.

But that young mother clearly had a death wish.

The hellish hound had gone about five metres when it suddenly squatted and deposited a foul-smelling pile in the middle of the path. When it had finished, dog and owner carried on walking. There was no attempt to scoop the poop.

The mother was incandescent. "Hey, you! Come back here and clear that up!" she yelled at the dog owner's back. "That's disgusting! It's a health hazard! You can be prosecuted for that!"

Her voice was so loud it carried clean across the park. Everyone looked at her. Everyone, that is, but the young man. He didn't turn. Didn't react at all. Just carried on walking.

"If you don't do something, I'll pick it up myself and shove it through your letter box," the mother screamed, purple with rage. "I can find out where you live. You lot are all the same. Dog owners! You think you own the park. You won't get away with it!"

I shivered. It was a hot day, but the atmosphere had become positively Arctic.

small packages

Graham and I didn't stop to see what happened next. Bertie started to wriggle, but Graham didn't dare set him down anywhere near the kids in case they started screaming again. We walked quickly in the opposite direction and only released Bertie when we were out of sight. But we soon realized that the path would carry us round in a big circle and we were likely to meet the horrible hoodie and his hellhound again. So we nipped out of the side gate near the shrubbery and cut down a back alley to the vet's to collect Bertie's eye-drops.

"That was all a bit weird, wasn't it?" I said. The vet's reception area was quite crowded, and as we stood in line waiting for our turn, I felt a bit shaky.

"It was rather odd," agreed Graham quietly. "I suppose the children must suffer from some sort of phobia. They certainly appeared to have an irrational aversion to dogs. As did their mother."

"Bertie's not exactly threatening, is he? Mind you, I didn't like the look of that mastiff thing."

"Nor did I. And his owner is definitely someone to avoid."

I was so distracted that the receptionist had to ask me twice to confirm Mrs Biggs's address before she'd give me Bertie's medication. Once I'd handed over the cash, we headed home.

We had to walk Bertie twice daily, regular as clockwork, without fail. Graham hung around at my house in between our park trips: it was just too hot to go anywhere or do anything else. I lounged about in the garden reading trashy thrillers and sipping chilled smoothies while Graham sat hunched over Mum's computer trying to figure out the precise connection between the current heatwave and long-term climate change.

Everything proceeded more or less smoothly for about a week. True, Bertie still wasn't keen on the actual journey to and from the park. Every time Graham and I turned up he regarded us with Deep Suspicion.

Graham ended up borrowing his neighbour's skate-board and converting it into a kind of doggy go-kart so we could pull Bertie along instead of breaking our backs carrying him everywhere.

Everything was fine, if a little dull. Then, on Saturday morning, things suddenly got nasty.

The walk itself was fairly uneventful. Bertie greeted all of his mates politely. Admittedly he'd then stolen Sam – the obsessive collie's – ball and made off with it under a bush. It had taken us nearly twenty minutes to persuade Bertie to come back out. Then we met Jessie, the golden retriever. She was accompanied by a fresh-faced, outdoorsy woman rather than the shaggy-haired surfer dude we'd met before. Jessie bounced around Bertie in great galumphing circles but he ignored her. Bertie had an important job to do: he was on a mission to rid the world of daisies. In an attempt to distract him, Jessie rolled over onto her back. It didn't work. Her owner – the surfer guy's wife, presumably – knelt down to scratch the dog's stomach consolingly. "Won't he play?" she laughed. "Poor Jessie!"

Just then the auburn-haired Super Speedy Sprinting Woman came pounding across the grass with her red setter. She was on a collision course with us, so I grabbed Bertie and we prepared to take evasive action.

However, when the runner saw Jessie she slowed

down and plucked the headphones out of her ears. I thought that maybe she was going to stop and talk, but when she saw the retriever was being walked by someone different, she carried on running.

Interesting, I thought. She'd stopped for a long chat with Surfer Dude only the day before, and yet she'd completely ignored his wife...

I glanced at Mrs Surfer Dude but she hadn't even noticed the sprinting woman. All of her attention was fixed on the back gate and her eyes had narrowed thoughtfully. Graham and I followed her gaze and saw that Mumsiewumsie had entered the park with Malcolm and Stanley.

Bertie didn't rate Jessie as a doggy friend, but he was mates with the shih tzu. Graham and I had learned enough about Bertie's habits by then to know that there would be no shifting him until he'd had a chance to sniff both dogs' bottoms. Jessie, it seemed, wanted a piece of the action too. She was wagging her tail so hard we were getting bruised knees.

Mumsiewumsie greeted me and Graham with, "How's Bertie's mum?"

Assuming she was referring to Mrs Biggs rather than Bertie's biological mother, I said, "She's fine. Bearing up, you know."

"Yes, I heard she'd had an accident," Mrs Surfer

Dude said, joining the conversation. "Awful. And in this heat, too! That plaster must be driving her mad. How long do they think she'll be laid-up?"

"Not sure," I said. To be honest, I hadn't really listened to the medical details.

But Graham had. "At least six weeks," he informed us. "Maybe longer, depending on how well the bone knits together."

Mumsiewumsie had pulled her treat box from her handbag. Scenting food, all four dogs sat down.

"Not you, Jessie!" Mrs Surfer Dude clapped the golden retriever onto a lead. "I need to watch her weight," she explained.

Bertie took his treat politely but Malcolm and Stanley snatched theirs as usual, despite another firm telling-off. "You're very bad boys, and them as don't behave won't be getting their Sunday lunch, will they? It's roast beef tomorrow. And you know how much you like my Yorkshire puddings, don't you, boys?" Both dogs looked blank. You'd have thought they couldn't understand a word she was saying.

"They love a roast," Mumsiewumsie told us confidentially. "No potatoes, mind. I won't give them those."

"Too fattening?" I asked, observing the dogs' complete lack of waistlines.

"No," she replied. "Gives them terrible wind."

Mrs Surfer Dude had been chewing her lip while Mumsiewumsie was talking. She looked as if she wanted to say something but couldn't find the right words. "That's a terrible diet!" she finally blurted out. "Really, it's so unhealthy. You'll make them ill."

"I beg your pardon?" said Mumsiewumsie frostily.

"I'm sorry, I didn't mean to be rude. It's just that..."

Mumsiewumsie drew herself up to her full height. She only came up to Mrs Surfer Dude's chin, but with immense dignity she said, "I'll thank you to keep your nose out of my private business. They're my boys and I'll feed them whatever I like."

Mumsiewumsie had the figure of an egg on legs, so she didn't exactly stride away in an epic fit of fury – it was more of a waddle and a huff – but it had the same effect.

Jessie's owner sighed and said to me and Graham, "Poor dogs. They're heading for heart attacks at this rate. Oh well. You win some, you lose some. See you around." And then she left too.

Bertie walked us for the forty-five minutes required by Mrs Biggs and then we headed home. Everything was fine until we led the Pekinese back through his front door.

The second Bertie's claws clicked on the tiled corridor

I knew something was seriously wrong. The television was switched off, for starters. The silence was deafening.

I looked at Graham. "Sounds ominous," I said nervously. I'd begun to think Mrs Biggs must have had another fall – maybe she'd been carted off to hospital again, or worse, maybe she was lying dead in the front room. But before my imagination could go into overdrive I heard Mum's voice calling from the kitchen, "Poppy, is that you?"

"Yes," I answered, confused. What was Mum doing here? And why did she sound so cross?

Graham and I followed Bertie down the corridor into the lounge, where Mrs Biggs fixed us with a Wounded Look. Mum was wearing a Stern Expression.

"What?" I said defensively. "What have we done?"

"It's more a matter of what you haven't," said Mum. "Look what came through Mrs Biggs's door while you were out."

When you've walked a dog twice a day for a whole week it doesn't take much to recognize a bag of poo – and there was one sitting on top of a Jiffy bag right in the middle of Mrs Biggs's coffee table.

"I don't get it…" I began.

"I told you what you needed to do," said Mrs Biggs. "It's not difficult."

I started to get angry. No one likes to be falsely

accused of doing something. Or not doing it. "I've scooped!" I protested.

Graham backed me up. "I assure you, Poppy has been most conscientious. Having witnessed her performing the task on several occasions, I can personally vouch for it."

"And you put it where you're supposed to – in the doggy bin?"

"Of course!" I said indignantly.

"How odd," said Mum. "Why would someone post something like that through the door? What a nasty thing to do..."

I couldn't agree more.

"Throw it away," she went on. "It's obviously just someone playing a silly joke. A malicious prank, that's all."

Gingerly picking the bag up by its handles, I dropped it back into the Jiffy bag and shoved it in the dustbin. I was unnerved by the whole thing, and judging from the look on Graham's face, he felt the same. Not that we had a chance to discuss the matter, as Mum was dragging me off to town for a spot of Back to School shopping, which – as you can imagine – I was thrilled about.

It wasn't until we took Bertie out for his walk that evening that Graham and I had a chance to talk.

"Do you think it could have been that mum? The

one with the screaming kids? I mean, she threatened that man – you know, the guy with the hoodie."

"Yes, she did. But he didn't clear up after his dog – unlike us. So why on earth would she send a package like that to Mrs Biggs?"

"I don't know. But she didn't like Bertie sitting down in that puddle. Maybe it was because of that. Even so, it's all a bit odd…"

When we got to the park we found a disconsolate pack of dog owners gathered on the grass. Mumsie-wumsie and Mrs Surfer Dude's argument had clearly been forgotten, because whoever was responsible for Mrs Biggs's mysterious package had been hard at work. Everyone had found similar parcels on their doormats. While the dogs played, their owners conversed in low, worried tones.

Mumsiewumsie was almost beside herself. "It were downright nasty, it were. Right there on the mat. Nearly stepped in it."

"It's outrageous. Something ought to be done," fretted Byron's bow-tie-wearing owner.

"I called the police," Mumsiewumsie told him. "I told my boys, I'm just not having it."

When Horrible Hoodie and his hellhound came along the path, the owners bunched together like angry sheep and began muttering about how some people shouldn't be allowed to keep dogs; some owners gave everyone else a bad name. Hoodie wasn't bothered – in fact, a nasty leer spread across his face. He looked like a Man Who Knew Something.

"I called the police too," Mrs Surfer Dude said in a low voice. "Grant thought I was overreacting, but ... well, it's just not nice, is it? It makes you feel so uneasy! And how did they know where we all live?"

Mumsiewumsie didn't answer. No one did. They all seemed lost for words and I could see why.

The dog crowd were clearly a pretty chatty bunch, but it was only their pets they talked about. I knew most of the dogs' names by now – their owners were always shouting them out, so it wasn't hard to remember. I also knew who each animal was friendly with, who they attacked on sight and what games they liked to play. On the other hand, I knew virtually nothing about their owners. I didn't know their names, and I most certainly didn't know any of their addresses. A worrying thought hit me. Could someone have been following owners home from the park? Had they done that to me and Graham?

Before I had a chance to say anything, Super Speedy Sprinting Woman bounded through the gate. The sight of such a large group of people gathered on the grass made her pause. She hesitated, running on the spot, as if wondering whether to come over. Her eyes flicked across the dogs. Located Jessie, the golden retriever. She glanced at the owners and saw Mrs Surfer Dude. That decided her: she ran on. But Ball Obsessed Collie Woman waved to her and beckoned. She had no choice.

Pulling the headphones from her ears as she approached the group, she said reluctantly, "What's the problem?"

"It's Alexandra, isn't it?" Collie Woman smiled placatingly. "I saw your name in the paper after you won that half-marathon."

"What's up?"

"It's just that … well … we all seem to have had a bit of a nasty surprise this morning. I wondered if you—"

"Yes, I got one too," she interrupted. "Some nutter. Best to ignore it."

And that was the extent of her conversation. Stuffing her headphones back in her ears, she and the inexhaustible red setter took off.

"You don't think it's Kath, do you?" Mrs Surfer Dude suddenly asked Collie Woman. "I couldn't bear it. Not after the business with Spike."

"No!" said Collie Woman, looking worried. "Surely not…"

"It couldn't be. That would be awful!" cried Mumsiewumsie.

"Spike?" I asked. "Who's Spike?"

Everyone fell silent. Mrs Surfer Dude's eyes were wide with anxiety. Mumsiewumsie picked up Malcolm in one arm and Stanley in the other, as if to protect them from some unseen danger. The ball-obsessed collie was brought to heel. Hamlet and Gertrude were clipped onto leads. One by one, the dog owners melted away, darting furtive, anxious glances over their shoulders as they left the park.

dermot o'flannery

The following morning an article appeared in the local paper. Mrs Surfer Dude must have called the news desk as well as the police, because there was a photo of her and her husband with Jessie on the front page, holding a bag of poo and looking disgusted. It was only then that I learnt their real names: Gabbie and Grant Robinson. He worked for an outdoor pursuits centre; she was employed by the RSPCA.

It must have been a very slack news day, because the next thing we knew the local TV station had sent a crew to cover the story. When we took Bertie for his morning walk we saw a car and a van parked on the tarmac near the park gates. A crowd had gathered to watch the excitement.

The presence of cameras might not in itself have been riveting, but the fact that the reporter was Dermot O'Flannery was enough to grab my attention.

"Look!" I said to Graham. "It's him."

"Who?" asked Graham.

"Dermot something. His wife got bashed by a burglar, do you remember? It was about six months ago, I think."

"Yes, it was." Graham frowned, trying to recall the details. "He went to pieces afterwards, didn't he?"

"Yes – threw himself into her grave at the funeral. And then he burst into tears on live TV while he was reading the headlines. It was dead embarrassing." I was vague on the precise details of the murder case, but I remembered that incident clearly enough – it had been a pitiful sight and afterwards he'd lost his job as the station's anchorman.

But it looked like he was beginning to scrape the shattered fragments of his life back together. He was clearly having to start at the very bottom of the career ladder again, though – doing an item on dog poo was hardly the cutting edge of investigative journalism.

Nevertheless, Dermot O'Flannery seemed extremely nervous. He looked pale and kept swallowing anxiously, as if he was about to interview an assembly of world leaders.

By the time Graham and I arrived at the park, a whole pack of interviewees had assembled. Byron's bow-tied owner was beating about in the bushes, although there was no sign of his beagle. Mumsiewumsie was sitting on a bench near by with Malcolm and Stanley, feeding them treats. Collie Woman was throwing a ball for Sam. The small Spanish woman with the large Great Dane was talking to the short, fat owner of the long, thin dachshund. One of the TV crew had jotted down their names and addresses and they were all ready and willing to tell Dermot their story, but he didn't seem very keen to begin.

Graham and I casually sidled over to Mr and Mrs Surfer Dude, aka Grant and Gabbie Robinson. I'd asked Mrs Biggs about the mysterious Spike incident but she'd only paled and said she didn't want to discuss it, so I was hoping to overhear something interesting. They were discussing Dermot O'Flannery, or at least, Gabbie Robinson was. Her husband was squatting down next to Jessie, both arms around the dog's neck. And he was watching Super Speedy Sprinting Woman as she ran around the perimeter of the park. His tongue was practically lolling out. I half expected him to start drooling.

Gabbie hadn't noticed her husband's preoccupied silence. Her back was to him and her eyes were fixed on the pale-but-undeniably-handsome TV presenter. "He doesn't look well, does he?" She sighed. "Mind you, after what that poor man's been through it's hardly surprising."

There was silence as both of them drifted along in their own little worlds. But then Gabbie Robinson's eyes fell on Mumsiewumsie. "That wretched woman! Look at her, stuffing those dogs full of treats. She'll make them clinically obese if she's not careful. They're already badly overweight. It's abuse, really: every bit as bad as neglecting them. You know, I've had a word with her but she just brushed me off! If things don't improve, I'll have to take action." She sighed again heavily. "Why can't people look after their animals properly?"

"If they did, you'd be out of a job," her husband said coldly. Alexandra had stopped running and seemed to be doing some stretching exercises before she left the park. "Jessie's getting bored sitting here," Grant added casually. "I'll just take her for a quick run."

"What about the interview?" demanded Gabbie.

"You can manage on your own, can't you? You always do." Grant didn't wait for an answer, and five seconds later he was chatting to the red-headed runner on the other side of the park while Jessie and the setter romped on the grass together.

By now the make-up girl had finished dabbing Dermot's nose, but there was no disguising the fact that his face was a nasty shade of ivory beige. Despite the powder, sweat had beaded on his forehead and he was saying weakly, "Why did it have to be this story? I don't want to do it. I asked them to let me cover the flower show!"

"I know," soothed the make-up girl, "but Brian was taken ill this morning. There wasn't anyone else available." She looked thoroughly worried. "Are you feeling OK, Dermot? Shall I get you some tea or something?"

The cameraman was more brutal. After checking his watch impatiently he said, "We need to get on. We've got to wrap this one up quickly or we won't get to the council offices on time. We're doing that piece about bin collections, remember?"

"Sure, of course, you're right." Dermot took a very deep breath and muttered to himself, "Come on, Dermot, act like a professional. You can do this."

Graham and I stood on the sidelines with Bertie and watched, but I have to say that the interviews Dermot carried out weren't exactly gripping. He talked to the assembled owners and they all said pretty much the same thing: about how shocked they were by the packages and how strange and unfair it was because they were responsible owners who always cleaned up after their dogs. "Unlike some," Gabbie Robinson added darkly as she caught sight of Horrible Hoodie being dragged along the path by his hellhound. Dermot followed her gaze and his own eyes narrowed as if he was wondering whether to interview him, too, but when the mastiff cocked a leg against the nearest tree, Dermot looked away, clearly changing his mind.

In order to flesh the item out, Dermot also got what he called "vox pops" from other park users about their opinion of urban dogs. When he came across the young mother of the screaming, dog-phobic kids in the play area, he must have thought he'd hit TV interviewer's gold.

She was as angry as she'd been when she had that go at Bertie, and kept raving about how disgusting it was when people didn't clear up after their animals and what nasty diseases small children could catch from dog poo and the terrible dangers of out-of-control canines and how every single one of them should be microchipped and licensed and never ever be walked off the lead in a public place because it just wasn't safe.

Dermot looked even paler when he'd finished talking to her, but that wasn't surprising – she was enough to intimidate anyone.

*　　*　　*

The crew were getting ready to leave and we were about to head for home when Bertie trundled up to Dermot and sniffed his shoes. For one dreadful moment I thought he was going to widdle on them, but instead he looked up at the news reporter, grinned a doggy grin and wagged his tail.

"Hello there, fella." Dermot smiled. Bertie continued to gaze up at him, so Dermot reached down to ruffle his coat. "Sure, you've a big personality for a little guy, haven't you?" he said.

"Do you have a dog?" Graham asked politely.

"No, I don't," replied Dermot, climbing into the front seat of his car and starting the engine. "I'm not that keen on them, to be honest. Guess I'm really more of a cat man."

Puzzling, I thought, watching him go. Very puzzling indeed. Dermot O'Flannery said he didn't have a dog.

So why was there a huge metal dog guard fixed across the boot of his car?

Graham and I watched the dog poo item on the evening news with Mum. The not-exactly-gripping series of interviews had been cut to make the piece quite interesting. And when the young mother came on, the screen caption informed us that her name was Kathryn Hughes.

I waited until the programme was over and Mum was safely in the kitchen starting on the tea before I said to Graham, "Do you remember what Gabbie Robinson said? Something about 'Kath'. Kathryn. Kath. Are they the same person?"

"Could be," said Graham.

"Can we find out more about her? And that 'business with Spike' that Gabbie mentioned?"

"Do you think Kathryn Hughes was responsible for those packages?" asked Graham.

"Well, you heard what she said to Horrible Hoodie," I replied, switching on the computer. "She certainly hates dogs. No one else would have that motive, would they? It's got to be her. It stands to reason." I typed her name into the search engine.

"Posting dog poo doesn't amount to much of a crime, though," Graham pointed out as I scrolled down through the zillion and one Kathryn Hughes that seemed to populate the world.

"No. But if she's gone a bit mad ... well, you never know how far someone like that will go, do you? She ought to be stopped."

Graham reached over, grabbed the mouse and clicked on the Google news icon. He found what we needed pretty much immediately. There was a report from the local paper dated a few months ago. It turned out that Kathryn Hughes's small son had been badly bitten by a friend's pet: a two-year-old Alsatian called Spike. The dog had been put down despite desperate pleas from its owners, Gabbie and Grant Robinson.

Graham breathed out slowly. It was a while before either of us said anything.

"Well, that explains why the kid screamed when Bertie surprised him," I said eventually.

"Yes," murmured Graham. "And it also explains why Kathryn Hughes is so vehemently anti-dog. And why she now regards the entire canine population as a potential threat."

"So what do you reckon? She's sending out those packages as some sort of revenge?"

Graham nodded. "It would seem to fit the facts. But surely she's not a real danger to anyone? It's unpleasant, that's all."

"You're probably right."

We crossed our fingers and told ourselves that Kathryn Hughes's anti-dog campaign was weird but basically harmless.

Except it wasn't.

While we were out walking Bertie on Monday morning another package plopped onto Mrs Biggs's mat, and this time there was a single word scrawled across the back of the Jiffy bag: DIE!

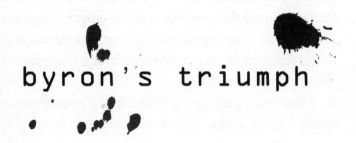

byron's triumph

We took Bertie for his evening walk at 5.30 p.m. As soon as we got through the gates we spotted Gabbie Robinson. She'd been throwing a stick for Jessie, but when she saw us she shouted, "Did Bertie's mum get another one too?"

I nodded. "With writing on it this time."

"Same here. Who'd do something like that?"

Ball Obsessed Collie Woman joined us, along with the Great Dane's small owner and the dachshund's fat one, and then Mumsiewumsie appeared and for the next ten minutes or so all the grown-ups had a good long moan about the nasty anonymous message. Hellhound was in the park too, along with his owner, who had his skull-embossed hoodie pulled well down over his face like he didn't want to talk to anyone. Not that anyone would have tried – all the other dog owners avoided him whenever possible. As he headed towards the shrubbery, no one called him over to see if he'd been sent a similar parcel.

There was a distinct frosting of the atmosphere a moment later, and I looked around to see what – or rather who – had caused it. Kathryn Hughes was coming down the path. The kids in the double buggy were fast asleep, which was probably just as well. Gabbie threw Kathryn a look so acid it could have melted through solid steel as the mother carried on walking in the same direction as Horrible Hoodie. Then, without warning, she suddenly exploded. "Silly cow!" she said. "If she'd controlled that kid of hers nothing would have happened!"

"What do you mean?" I asked.

Gabbie Robinson fixed me with a furious stare. "You try sticking your fingers in your eyes, see how it makes you feel! If her kid had kept his hands to himself, my Spike would never have bitten him!"

She looked on the verge of tears. Then she turned and strode off, whistling to Jessie and following the same path that Kathryn Hughes had taken. I hoped she wouldn't catch up. I'd have bet all my pocket money that if those two women met, a fist fight would break out in thirty seconds flat.

There was an embarrassed silence, and after a few mumbled goodbyes and half-hearted waves the crowd of dog owners dispersed.

Bertie, however, had decided to weed that particular section of lawn. He'd conquered the daisies but had now found a new enemy to vanquish: dandelions. We knew from experience that there was absolutely no point trying to get him to follow us while he was working on a project, so Graham and I sat on a bench to keep an eye on him. From there we had a good view of most of the park.

Ball Obsessed Collie was hurtling back and forth, doing his thing with the ball. Mumsiewumsie was strolling towards the back gate. She took the long route around the shrubbery and was soon out of sight. Horrible Hoodie, Kathryn Hughes and Gabbie Robinson had disappeared along the path that wove through the bushes.

Super Speedy Sprinting Woman came in through the main gate and started her usual circuit. She stopped, though, when Grant Robinson – who was possibly looking for his wife and dog, or possibly not – appeared behind her. The two of them proceeded to have an animated conversation in the middle of the grass, punctuated by so many bursts of laughter that they drew disapproving glances from the small Spanish woman and the owner of the dachshund. If Bertie had been a more co-operative dog we might have managed to sidle over for a spot of eavesdropping, but I knew there was no chance of that.

Horrible Hoodie must have changed his mind about going through the shrubbery, because it wasn't long before he was heading back towards us, his hellhound straining on its length of chain.

By now it was nearly 6 p.m. Gabbie Robinson had reached the side gate and was about to leave when Jessie suddenly went galumphing off into the undergrowth, not paying the slightest attention to her owner's shouts. So Gabbie went in pursuit.

At 6.15 p.m. precisely Bertie's in-built clock told him it was time for tea. He executed his last dandelion and trundled over to us expectantly. Graham and I prepared to escort His Lordship home.

But then Byron the runaway beagle dashed past, tail stiff as a paintbrush, nose glued to the ground, on the trail of what appeared to be the most irresistible scent he'd ever detected.

"Do you need a hand?" we asked his desperate owner as he hobbled breathlessly after him, flat cap in one hand, tweed jacket in the other, bow tie askew.

"Could you? I'd be so grateful. He's heading for the rhododendrons. Maybe you could cut him off at the pass."

Carrying Bertie under one arm and the doggy go-kart under the other, Graham slipped down one side of the bushes while I nipped around the back and Byron's owner approached from the far end. All three of us reached the clearing at the same time.

Byron was standing proudly, tail wagging frantically. The hound clearly thought he had done the best day's tracking of his entire life. His tongue was hanging out of a widely grinning mouth and he looked like he was expecting a medal.

He'd led us all straight to Mrs Surfer Dude. Gabbie Robinson was lying face down, arms at her sides, almost as if she was asleep in the sun.

But the back of her head had been caved in with a single, vicious blow. Her death must have been instant.

give the dog
a bone

It wasn't a pretty sight.

We stood there, frozen, for a few seconds. Then Byron's owner grabbed his bow tie as if it was choking him. He ripped it off and started throwing up into the nearest bin. Graham handed Bertie to me and called the police on his mobile.

Jessie, meanwhile, was lying beside her owner, oblivious to the drama. She had an extremely large joint of meat clutched between her paws – the kind of thing you'd roast for a Sunday dinner. She was still chewing on it happily when the police arrived, and was very put out when one of them prised it from her mouth and dropped it into an evidence bag.

Graham and I were delighted to find out that Inspector Humphries was on holiday. We didn't think he'd be too thrilled to discover that we were the first to arrive at yet another crime scene. We hadn't met Inspector Fowler before, and she must have been new to the area, because when she saw me and Graham she frowned and said to the nearest constable, "Why didn't you tell me there were children involved? This is a most unsuitable place for them. Take them home immediately."

Byron's owner was in a far worse state than either of us, but he was a grown-up, so it was left to him to fill her in on what had happened. We were carted off in a panda car with Bertie, who was terribly indignant about the delay to his tea. After handing him back to Mrs Biggs, we went over to my house to give PC Trevor Black our statement while Mum quietly fumed from the armchair about our uncanny ability to get ourselves involved in murder investigations.

We told PC Black all we'd seen and noticed. When we mentioned Horrible Hoodie changing direction and coming back past us, he looked up from his notebook.

"You sure?" he asked. "You saw Kyle Jacobs? Black sweatshirt, skull motifs, big dog?"

We nodded in unison.

He scratched his head and flipped back a few pages.

"It's just that the woman with the two little dogs…"

"Mumsiewumsie?" we filled in helpfully.

"Mrs Braithwaite," he said sternly. "She said she saw him leaving through the back gate at about ten past six. Mind you," he added with a roll of the eyes that spoke volumes about the reliability of most witnesses, "she couldn't swear if that was today, yesterday or last week." He shut his notebook with a decisive thwack. "It will be easy enough to check his movements, though. The guy's tagged."

My ears pricked up at this.

"Tagged?" Mum asked, alarmed. "You mean he's been in trouble with the police? Is he dangerous?"

"Oh no, ma'am. No need to concern yourself about him. There was an incident a few months ago. Minor theft. Nothing too serious. Rest assured, we're keeping an eye on him."

Mum didn't look terribly reassured, but there wasn't much more the policeman could say or do. When the panda car pulled away, Mum insisted on driving Graham home. Every so often she would look over her shoulder as if expecting hoodies to come bursting out from behind a bush. When we reached his house, she escorted him up the path and shoved him through his door without stopping for her usual chat with his mum, Sally. It was all so quick that Graham and I didn't even get a chance to say goodbye. It wasn't until later – when Mum was fast asleep and I was tucked up in bed with the mobile phone I'd cunningly removed from her coat pocket – that we could talk things over.

"What do you reckon?" I said. "It's got to be Kathryn, hasn't it?"

"It certainly looks highly likely," Graham answered slowly. "As far as I can see, she was the only one with the motive, means and opportunity. Mothers can be extremely dangerous when it comes to defending their young. I suppose the incident with Spike must have turned her thoughts to murder."

"She really hated Gabbie Robinson," I agreed. "She could easily have hidden in the bushes. The kids were fast asleep. And she had that big bag on the pushchair. I guess the murder weapon was in that. And the meat. No wonder Jessie ran off – she must have caught a whiff of it. Lure the dog in and the owner's bound to follow. All Kathryn had to do was wait."

"If it was Kathryn, and I'm inclined to think it must have been – that might put Gabbie's husband in danger. He was Spike's owner too."

"Grant Robinson? I bet he feels dead guilty now," I said.

"Why?" asked Graham.

"Well, there he was, flirting with Super Speedy

Sprinting Woman while his wife was getting killed just a hundred metres away." And remembering the way the two of them had been chatting, I added, "You know, I reckon that sprinter has a thing for him. She's always really friendly when she sees him. But when it's Gabbie walking Jessie, not Grant, she never even stops to say hello. She'd have a motive for murder, wouldn't she?"

"Gabbie must have been killed between 6 p.m. – when we last saw her – and 6.15 p.m. when we found her corpse," objected Graham. "Alexandra and Grant were talking the entire time. We sat and watched them. She may have had a motive, but she certainly didn't have an opportunity."

"I suppose so. I guess we can rule both of them out, then."

We talked for a bit longer but didn't come up with anything else. The dog-phobic young mother was the only person in the park who had the motive, means *and* opportunity. As far as we could see, the case against Kathryn Hughes was an open-and-shut one.

I really hate those.

bad news

There may have been a murderer on the loose, but
Mrs Biggs still had a broken leg and Bertie still needed
exercise. However, now things had turned nasty Mum
insisted on coming to the park with us.

The next day there were lots of police in and around
the shrubbery, and then – surprise, surprise – a TV
crew arrived with a squeal of tyres to cover the lat-
est gruesome developments. When Dermot O'Flannery
climbed out of his car, Mum did her hair flicking thing
and moved towards him, a friendly smile playing across
her lips.

He gave her a quick nod, a wink and a grin – the

professional reaction of a TV personality to a fan.

We watched while he did a serious piece to camera, explaining how RSPCA inspector Gabbie Robinson had been brutally murdered in the park. Then he talked to Mumsiewumsie, who was in tears throughout the interview, and Collie Woman, whose voice was husky with shock. The small Spanish lady wailed about how terrible it was, and the short, fat man did a lot of sighing and tutting and fretting about how nowhere was safe any more. Byron's owner refused point-blank to do an interview – he was far too traumatized, he said. It was all too awful: he'd never let his beagle off the lead again for fear of what he might find.

After Dermot had completed the interviews, he shed his earnest manner like a winter coat and grinned at Bertie as the Pekinese trundled towards him, tail wagging.

"Hello again there, little fella." He bent down to stroke him. "Sure, you're a friendly one, aren't you?"

"Isn't he just?" said Mum, stepping in front of me and Graham with an eagerness that was downright embarrassing. "Bertie loves people."

"So is he your dog?" Dermot asked, looking Mum up and down in a way that made her blush with pleasure. "You don't look the Pekinese type."

"No ... he belongs to our neighbour. My daughter

and her friend have been exercising him for her. She's got a broken leg."

"A broken leg?" Dermot's journalistic instincts stood to attention. It was like watching Byron catch a distant whiff of fox. "An accident, was it? Or deliberate? Was it linked with the other incidents?"

"Oh no, no, no," said Mum hastily. "Mrs Biggs tripped. One of those silly accidents, you know?"

"Ah, OK." Dermot was losing interest, so Mum added eagerly, "But Poppy and Graham were the ones to discover the body!"

Oh, so suddenly me and Graham getting mixed up in Violent Deaths wasn't so bad after all! Outrageous.

"Were they now?" Dermot's eyes narrowed. It was like being stared at by a man with X-ray vision. "Mind if I have a word, then?"

So Graham and I had to do an interview too. It was exceedingly brief – we knew full well that we weren't allowed to give any actual details about what we'd seen in case it interfered with the police investigation. All we could do was murmur softly about how upsetting it was, which was perfectly true. When I saw myself on the news later I looked devastated. But what was really bothering me wasn't so much Gabbie Robinson's death: it was how we were going to shake Mum off so Graham and I could investigate properly. I don't believe in open-and-shut cases. I knew in my bones that there had to be more to it – and Graham and I were both determined to find out what.

After we'd returned Bertie to Mrs Biggs, Mum took Graham and me to the swimming-pool. Our parents had agreed that while *they* were working *we* needed to be taken to a safe public place and left there. Mum escorted us into the lobby of the sports centre with strict instructions to go straight to the pool and remain in the water until she came back.

"I'll tap on the glass," she said. "I want to see you in there, OK? No running about poking your noses in where they're not wanted. I've only got a few lawns to mow; I'll be an hour. Two at the most. You're not to leave the building, got it?"

We nodded meekly and pushed our way through the turnstiles. But instead of heading straight to the changing-rooms, we hid around the corner until Mum had gone. Then we doubled back to the lobby and set off up the stairs to the Internet café, which was oh-so-conveniently located on the first floor.

"So," I said, sipping a Coke, "is Kathryn Hughes our number-one suspect?"

"She has to be," said Graham. "We saw for ourselves how emotionally volatile she is."

"There have got to be other suspects, though. Who might want to get rid of Gabbie Robinson? I still reckon Super Speedy Sprinting Woman and Gabbie's husband had motives."

"But not the means or the opportunity. We have to rule them out," Graham said wisely.

"Who else, then? Didn't Dermot say Gabbie was an RSPCA inspector? She could have had lots of enemies."

"He did."

"How do they work? Is it like social services?"

"What do you mean?"

"Well, if someone's not looking after their pet properly, could Gabbie take it into care?"

"I believe that would be possible."

"So…" I reasoned. "Maybe Gabbie was involved in cruelty cases or something. She might have been responsible for taking someone's pet away from them. Hey! She could have had it put down if it was like a dangerous dog or something. She might have had loads of chances to upset people. Let's look her up."

The first thing we discovered about Gabbie was that she'd been the judge in a local dog show at the start of the summer holidays. For a moment I wondered if that might have given someone a motive for killing her. But it wasn't exactly Crufts: the classes were things like "cutest puppy", "waggiest tail", "biggest smile" and "dog the judge would most like to take home". It didn't look like the sort of competition to inspire murderous rivalries.

Then, as Graham scrolled down, we came across something a whole lot more sinister.

Gabbie had been involved in some hideous animal cruelty cases, ranging from mild neglect to savage violence. Some of the photos we found made my stomach turn: wounded cats, starved dogs, blinded rabbits. There's something sick about hurting an animal that can't fight back.

From what we could see, Gabbie had prosecuted some truly evil people and several more cases were pending. There was one against a man who'd kept twenty-seven horses on a piece of land that wasn't much bigger than my back garden; a photo showed the poor things standing ankle-deep in mud, hips and ribs sticking up through their matted coats, eyes glazed and despairing. Another case involved a young man who was being prosecuted for shooting neighbourhood cats with a crossbow. A third "ongoing investigation" concerned a suspected dogfighting ring. As far as we could see, Gabbie could have had hundreds of enemies.

And yet, when I thought back to the evening Gabbie had died, I recalled that there hadn't been many people around.

"Do you reckon we'd have noticed someone unfamiliar?" I asked.

"It's a public place," replied Graham. "There could have been any number of complete strangers there."

"I know. But *were* there?" It occurred to me again that anyone who visited the park had a very particular reason for going. They all fitted into one category or another: dog walkers; joggers; young mums with kids; teenage gangs; old folk. Very occasionally a lone adult might take a short cut through it, but they always headed very purposefully from one side to the other.

"Whoever attacked Gabbie must have hung around for a while waiting for the chance to bash her over the head," I said. "But I didn't notice anyone out on their own – without a kid or a dog, I mean. I reckon they'd have stood out like a sore thumb. Anything out of the ordinary attracts attention in the park. Look what happened when the TV crew arrived."

"If you're right, the attacker would have had to be someone we're familiar with, at least by sight. Possibly one of the dog walkers?"

I flipped through them in my head. There was only one person, apart from Kathryn Hughes, who might have been in the right place at the right time. "Mumsie-wumsie," I said slowly. "We don't know where she was when Gabbie died. We couldn't see her, could we?"

"Are you suggesting she could have done it?"

"I don't know … maybe. Gabbie was worried about Malcolm and Stanley's weight. And she told Grant she was going to take action, didn't she?"

"Yes, she did." Graham looked thoughtful. "In fact, as I recall, Gabbie described their overfeeding as a form of abuse."

We eyed each other.

"Abuse," I repeated. "So Gabbie – as an RSPCA inspector – might have threatened to take Malcolm and Stanley away? I bet that wouldn't have gone down well with Mumsiewumsie."

Graham saw exactly where my thoughts were heading. "I read somewhere that according to a recent survey, many people are more attached to their pets than their relatives. As we've observed, Mumsiewumsie's terribly protective of Malcolm and Stanley. She treats them like her own offspring."

"And mothers are fierce when it comes to defending their young," I added. "If Gabbie was planning on taking those two shih tzu away … well, anything might have happened."

crash-landing

Once we'd finished our Cokes we headed to the changing-rooms to put on our swimming gear. We'd barely had time to get ourselves convincingly wet when Mum tapped on the glass in the viewing gallery.

There was nothing we could actually do about our suspicions. Mum had appointed herself our personal security guard, so there was no way we could even talk about it any more, let alone phone the police. In any case, we doubted they'd be interested in our theory unless we could produce some solid proof.

All three of us walked Bertie again that evening, Mum sticking so close to me and Graham that it felt like we were all grafted together at the hip.

We kept our eyes peeled for Mumsiewumsie but she didn't arrive at her usual time, which was odd – her routine had seemed pretty fixed up until then. Graham and I exchanged puzzled looks but didn't say anything.

Dogs need exercise no matter what, and we hadn't been in the park long before we noticed Jessie, bounding back and forth over the grass while an extremely white-faced Grant threw a stick for her. Every time she brought it back, he hugged her as if his life depended on it. Mum, not being much of an animal lover, didn't pay them any attention. All dogs look the same to her and she wasn't to know that Grant was the grieving widower. On the other hand, she did notice Super Speedy Sprinting Woman thudding towards us.

"Crikey! She's a bit stunning, isn't she? Amazing hair," said Mum, herding us to the edge of the path. "She was here yesterday, wasn't she?"

"She's here every day," I replied. "Morning and evening, like the rest of us, regular as clockwork."

Super Sprinter whizzed past, but something happened to her when she saw Grant. It was like watching a plane crash. The red setter was running rings around her as usual, but as soon as Alexandra spotted Jessie's owner she stopped dead. Her own dog bowled into her, knocking her clean off her feet. She fell forward onto the tarmac and there was suddenly blood gushing from her knees.

Every single person who saw the accident rushed at once to her aid, including me, Mum and Graham. Grant was the only one who didn't move towards her. Either he hadn't seen her trip – which seemed totally impossible – or he was too wrapped up in his own problems to care about anyone else.

While Mum dabbed at the bloody knees with a tissue and Ball Obsessed Collie Woman wondered aloud whether she ought to call an ambulance or drive her to A & E, Alexandra's eyes kept flicking across to Grant. At first there was a kind of furious anger in them, but as it became increasingly obvious that he wasn't coming over, her expression changed to one of confusion followed by Deep Distress. Her lower lip started to tremble and tears spilt down her lovely cheeks.

"Oh dear," fretted Mum. "You must be in shock. I really think you ought to get some medical attention – these cuts are quite deep."

"I thought he liked me!" Alexandra sobbed.

"Ah…" Mum oozed instant sympathy. Man problems? She was an expert on that subject. "You need a cup of tea, sweetheart. Let's get you to the café, shall we?"

Alexandra looked at Mum and clearly decided the prospect of Tea and Sympathy was irresistible. "But I've got Paddy," she said weakly, indicating the red setter. "I can't go in the café with him."

"Poppy and Graham will look after him, won't you?" said Mum. It wasn't a question, it was an order.

So Graham and I spent the next half hour standing outside the café, desperately trying to eavesdrop. We could only hear the odd phrase from Alexandra: "I thought we were friends, you know? A married man… I should have known better… He was using me…"

Mum's voice flowed in a soothing murmur between Alexandra's sentences. It was all deeply frustrating – and deeply odd, too. Mum and Alexandra had never met before. So why was Alexandra pouring her heart out to a complete stranger?

When Alexandra and Mum had finished their pot of tea, they started to make Better Get Going gestures at each other. There was still no sign of Mumsiewumsie.

"Do you think something's happened to her?" I asked Graham.

"Possibly. It does seem odd that she hasn't walked Malcolm and Stanley. Perhaps one of the other dog walkers knows something." I noticed that Ball Obsessed Collie Woman was about to leave the park. If we wanted to ask her any questions, it was now or never. She was too far away for me to attempt a casual greeting, so

I accidentally-on-purpose dropped Paddy's lead, hoping that he'd make a beeline for Sam the collie. If they sniffed noses – and, inevitably, bottoms – maybe I'd get the opportunity for a quick chat with Sam's owner.

Unfortunately, the minute Paddy felt the lead drop he took off, hurtling across the grass with such reckless abandon that I didn't have a hope of catching him. I screamed his name but the dog completely ignored me. He galloped past the collie and away into the distance. All I had achieved by my frantic yelling was to alert Alexandra to the fact that her dog had escaped from me. She leapt to her feet looking furious. Useless though it was, I set off in pursuit.

Luckily for me, Collie Woman was fully equipped to cope with Canine Emergencies. When she saw what had happened she pulled a treat box from her handbag and rattled it.

Every dog in the park heard and responded accordingly. Byron dragged his owner across the grass on his new extending lead, Hamlet and Jessie bounded towards her and Gertrude sped over as fast as her short legs could carry her. Meanwhile, Paddy had reappeared from the other side of the park. He circled her once, twice, and then came in like a homing pigeon. Collie Woman grabbed his lead.

"Thanks," I puffed.

"No problem."

Mum and Alexandra were fast approaching.

"Have you see Mums … er … Malcolm and Stanley's owner today?" I asked quickly.

Collie Woman frowned in concern. "No. I wonder where she's got to? It's unusual for her to miss her walk. I hope the dogs are OK."

I couldn't say any more without risking Mum's wrath, but my mind went into overdrive. I knew that Mumsiewumsie always came and left the park through the back gate. If we headed in that direction we might hear or see something interesting. But first I had to persuade Mum to go home by a different route. As she was saying her goodbyes to Alexandra, I remembered the shops near the rear entrance. There was a café and a hairdressers, neither of which was remotely useful. But there was a newsagent's, too…

I gave Graham a Significant Look and set off.

"Where are you going?" asked Mum. "Home's that way."

"But Mrs Biggs asked us to get her a paper," I said innocently.

"Did she?" Mum looked puzzled.

"Yes," I said firmly. "Weren't you listening?"

Mum flushed. I knew perfectly well that she let most of what Mrs Biggs said wash clean over her. All I had to do to convince her was to tut and roll my eyes at Graham.

We got more than I'd bargained for at the newsagent's. Mum picked up a copy of the local paper and stood in the queue to pay for it while Graham and I hovered in the background with Bertie. It took some time for Mum to get served because the man behind the counter was chatting to a pair of customers, both of whom had witnessed a nasty car accident earlier on that day.

Mumsiewumsie was in hospital, fighting for her life.

It seemed that she had stepped out in front of a car. The driver hadn't stopped. It had all happened so quickly that the two witnesses disagreed about the make and model and even the colour of the vehicle. But they both agreed on one thing.

There had been a dog guard fixed across the boot.

rescue dogs

Mrs Biggs was extremely upset when she heard about Mumsiewumsie's accident. "Hospital?" she said. "Oh my goodness! Is she badly hurt? Poor Doreen!" And then, a millisecond later, "Her boys! Who's looking after Malcolm and Stanley?"

We didn't have a clue – no one had mentioned them in the newsagent's. Mrs Biggs immediately swung into action. From her armchair she made about a million phone calls to various friends and acquaintances. Eventually she tracked Malcolm and Stanley to the vet's. Thinking they might have sustained internal injuries in the smash, a passing stranger had taken them there after Mumsiewumsie had been loaded into an ambulance.

Mrs Biggs called the vet and discovered that Malcolm and Stanley were fine – physically, at any rate. According to her we couldn't possibly leave them there overnight – all dogs are terrified of vets, she assured us. The mental distress Malcolm and Stanley would suffer would be appalling. She wasn't going to allow it. And neither were we. Mum, Graham and I were despatched on a Canine Rescue Mission. Our goal? To retrieve the shih tzu and deliver them safely into Mrs Biggs's care.

The rescue mission was easy enough. The little dogs were ridiculously pleased to see me and Graham, and pathetically grateful to be taken away from the Big Bad Vet. They trotted along at our heels, tails held high, all the way back to Mrs Biggs's house.

When we got there, we discovered we had another task to complete. We had to go to Mumsiewumsie's house and collect Malcolm and Stanley's personal possessions: food, treats, toys and beds.

"I need to get the tea on," protested Mum. "It's getting late."

But when it came to Canine Welfare, the usually mild-mannered Mrs Biggs had an edge of steel. "It won't take more than five minutes," she said firmly. "She lives at forty-one Leeds Street. It's only round the corner. Her neighbour's got a key – he'll let you in. Go on, dear. The poor loves won't settle otherwise."

Mum looked at her watch. Her stomach rumbled noisily and mine and Graham's joined in. We sounded like a chorus of frogs. "Graham and I can do it, Mum," I offered. "You get started on the food while we nip over. We don't need to go through the park – we can cut through the side streets. We'll be perfectly safe."

Mum wasn't happy, but she was hungry. We all were. Very. "OK, then," she sighed. "But be quick and no hanging about anywhere. Take my mobile just in case. Give me a call if you need me."

Mrs Biggs had underestimated the length of time it would take for us to reach Mumsiewumsie's house. It was a good ten-minute walk, and once there we had to stand on her neighbour's doorstep for ages while he found the key and then bored us to death by telling us how dreadful it all was and how dangerous drivers should be imprisoned or at least have their driving licences taken away from them and if he had his way no one under the age of thirty would ever be permitted behind a steering-wheel. He fixed Graham with an accusing look. "I bet it was a young man in that car. Dangerous, they are. Reckless. Unreliable. Shouldn't be allowed." It seemed very unfair: Graham is hardly the mad, reckless, daredevil type – and besides, he can't drive – but he didn't protest. There didn't seem to be any point.

It was another twenty minutes before we got inside the house, and then we had to find everything on Mrs Biggs's list. Mum called me on the mobile in a panic. As I reassured her that we hadn't been murdered, I surveyed the front room. Malcolm and Stanley's puppy photos were on the mantelpiece. In fact, pictures of the dogs adorned every available inch of space: Malcolm and Stanley on the beach; Malcolm and Stanley in the park; Malcolm and Stanley at Christmas; Malcolm and Stanley sharing their first birthday cake; Malcolm and Stanley sitting in high-chairs, eating their Sunday dinner.

When Mum had finished worrying, Graham and I searched the house for the dogs' gear. It wasn't hard to find. Malcolm and Stanley's names were hand-painted on the rims of two delicate bone china food bowls in the kitchen. They were neatly embroidered across two enormous floor cushions in the bedroom. They even had their own little velvet winter coats hanging up in the hall, their names picked out in diamanté studs.

"Well at least they won't be needing these," I told Graham. "It's far too hot for coats."

"True," said Graham earnestly. "But they may need their swimming trunks. I expect they're around here somewhere." He shot me another of his blink-and-you-miss-it grins.

We gathered up everything we thought Mrs Biggs might find useful, including a carrier bag full of the most expensive individually foil-wrapped meaty chunks money could buy.

"Well, we were right about one thing," I said as we pulled the door shut behind us. "She treats them like her children."

"Spoilt children," said Graham. "I don't have a hand-painted cereal bowl, do you?"

"No. Or a diamanté-embossed velvet coat."

We dropped the key back through the neighbour's letter box and headed home. "What do we reckon?" I asked Graham. "Do we still think she might have killed Gabbie Robinson?"

"I must admit, I find it hard to picture her cold-bloodedly striking Gabbie Robinson over the head."

"Same here. And what about the car accident? It was a deliberate attack," I said confidently. "Someone drove into her, I can just feel it."

"It could be a coincidence," Graham pointed out. "I gather that the number of hit-and-run incidents is on the increase."

"Two dog owners attacked in less than a week? No … something weird's going on. They've got to be connected. In which case, Mumsiewumsie's off the hook as far as Gabbie's murder is concerned." I stopped to readjust my load. Malcolm and Stanley's stuff was extremely heavy. "The car that hit her had a dog guard across it. You know, Dermot O'Flannery had one of those."

"Along with hundreds and thousands of other people."

"Yes, but he claims not to have a dog. He told us he's more of a cat man. So why the guard?"

"It could be perfectly innocent. He could have purchased the car second-hand, for example," suggested Graham. "It might not even have been his vehicle – it could be a staff car belonging to the TV station."

"True." I sighed. "Why would anyone hurt Mumsiewumsie? Do you reckon she might have seen something?"

"PC Black said she'd seen Kyle Jacobs leaving the park by the back gate. But that's not possible, as we know."

"So what reason could anyone have for wanting Mumsiewumsie out of the way? It doesn't make sense."

It was late but it was still hot and airless, and what with the armloads of cushions and bowls and food and toys, it wasn't long before we were too puffed-out to talk. By the time we staggered up Mrs Biggs's path we were faint with hunger. Next door, Mum had got the barbecue going, and as we arranged the cushions to Malcolm and Stanley's satisfaction and unwrapped meaty chunks for their tea, the smell of chargrilled sausages drifted over the fence. I started drooling like Kyle's hellhound.

"I called the hospital again," Mrs Biggs told us as we left. "Poor Doreen's got three cracked ribs and a dislocated shoulder. She's concussed, too, but they say she's sleeping quietly now. All things considered, it could have been worse."

When did we finally manage to sink our teeth into our sausages, I couldn't stop thinking about the accident.

Mrs Biggs was right. It could have been a lot worse. If the driver of that car had succeeded, Mumsiewumsie wouldn't be sleeping quietly in intensive care. She'd be lying on a slab in the mortuary.

arresting
developments

In the morning, Mum accompanied me and Graham
– and Bertie, Malcolm and Stanley – to the park. We
hadn't been there for more than five minutes when
the TV crew arrived in the shrubbery. The police had
removed their crime tape and Dermot was preparing to
do his piece to camera. The make-up girl was dabbing
at him with a powder puff and smoothing his hair into
place. He was standing on the exact spot where Graham
and I had found Gabbie's body.

Now, like I said, Mum has Big Objections when
it comes to us being involved in murder investigations, but these seemed to shrink into Such Tiny Little
Objections That They Don't Really Exist At All when

Dermot O'Flannery was within sniffing distance. Mum headed for him like a beagle on a trail, and she wasn't the only one. The TV star was attracting attention from all across the park. Even Grant Robinson, who was out walking Jessie again, was watching him.

Despite the make-up girl declaring him to be in a presentable condition, Dermot still checked his hair and teeth in a hand mirror before he started his piece.

"Friend or foe?" he said earnestly to the camera. "Reliable companion or dangerous nuisance? Love them or hate them, the subject of urban dogs arouses great passions on both sides of the debate. And here, on this very spot, passions became so inflamed that they led to violence. This morning police charged local mother-of-two Kathryn Hughes with the murder of Gabbie Robinson."

Gasps rippled around the onlookers. I glanced at Grant Robinson to see his reaction. He looked pained but not shocked – I suppose the police must have told him about it beforehand.

But as far as the other dog walkers were concerned this was major news. "Dios!" exclaimed the small Spanish woman, clutching Hamlet's neck for support. Gertrude's owner squeezed her so hard she started to yelp and wriggle. Ball Obsessed Collie Woman let out a low moan. Graham and I exchanged glances but didn't say anything. We didn't want Mum to remember her Responsible Adult duties and hurry us away.

The noise from the assembled crowd had been fairly muted, but it was enough to mean that Dermot had to re-record his bit. For the next take we were all ushered further away so no one could possibly be a distraction. We were elbowed aside by bigger, nosier people, and while Mum remained at the front of the group of onlookers, Graham and I ended up pretty much at the back. It would have been annoying if it wasn't for the fact that Horrible Hoodie – aka Kyle Jacobs – chose that moment to make an appearance.

He was wearing his usual top and the dog was on its usual chain, but on this occasion it was sporting a badly torn ear. It had been stitched up, but there was no disguising the fact that it was a serious injury. The pair of them were a scary sight.

Graham shuddered and picked up Bertie. Malcolm and Stanley cowered behind his legs. But curiosity got the better of me. Mum's attention was all on Dermot, so I turned around and smiled at Horrible Hoodie.

He did a kind of double take – I guess people didn't often grin at him. "Hi." I nodded towards his dog's tattered ear. "Nasty cut," I said sympathetically.

"Been in a fight," he said.

"Oh? Does he do that a lot?"

"Nah. Soft as butter, he is. He only done it coz something went for 'im." His voice was squeakier than I'd expected – rusty, almost – as if he didn't get the chance to use it much. He glanced at Dermot. "What's he doing here, then?"

"Breaking news," I said. "They've arrested Kathryn Hughes. You know, that young mum?"

"Oh, her." He grinned wickedly. "She done it, did she? She was a right old cow."

I changed the subject. "Did you get one of those poo packages through your door too?"

All of a sudden Kyle looked both extremely shifty and extremely amused. "Yeah, course I did." He sniffed loudly. "All got one, didn't we?" He was trying but failing to hide a malicious smirk. I threw the smallest of Significant Looks at Graham. I could see he was thinking the same as me: Kyle was lying. At that moment I'd have sworn that not only did he *not* get one, but that he was responsible for posting the bags in the first place. His eyes had virtually admitted as much.

"One?" I said. "Mrs Biggs got two. The second one had writing on it."

"Did she?" He looked puzzled. "Writing? What did it say?"

"*Die.*"

"You what?"

"*Die.* That's what it said. Didn't you get a second one too?"

"No. Yeah. I... Course I did." He fell silent.

Mum was still fixated with Dermot, but at any second she might turn round to check on us and then my conversation with Horrible Hoodie would come to a sudden end. I had one more important question to ask.

"Did you see anything the other night? I mean, when Mrs Surf— Gabbie Robinson was killed?"

"What?" He was startled by my change of tack. "What you on about?"

"Well, you were there in the shrubbery, weren't you? Before you came back past us. Did you see anything odd?"

"I weren't," he said hotly, fixing me with an angry stare. "I come straight through the side gate. I weren't nowhere near them bushes."

It was really odd. There could be no doubt at all that he was lying through his teeth. We'd seen him going in there ourselves! But if I hadn't known that – if I hadn't watched him with my very own eyes – I'd have sworn that he was telling the truth.

Once she'd heard about Kathryn Hughes's arrest, Mum decided to relax her self-imposed minder duties. After Dermot had finished his report and climbed into his car to leave, Mum suddenly realized she had A Million and One Better Things To Do than walk one reluctant Pekinese and two overweight shih tzu. She went home, leaving me and Graham to exercise the dogs.

"I reckon Horrible Hoodie posted those packages, don't you?" I asked.

"He certainly had the appearance of a guilty man," Graham agreed grimly. "I've never seen anyone look so shifty."

"How did he know everyone's addresses, though? I mean, we'd have noticed if he'd followed us home, wouldn't we? He's not exactly the kind of person you can miss."

Graham shrugged as if the answer was obvious. "There are other ways. You had to give Mrs Biggs's address when you picked up Bertie's eye-drops, if you recall. One would only have to sit in the vet's waiting-room and listen to obtain that kind of information."

"Oh … yeah, I see. I wonder why he did it, though? No one seems to like him much. Maybe he was just getting his own back."

Graham nodded. "The packages may have been his idea of a joke; something that came into his mind after the encounter between him and Kathryn Hughes. If so, it was just a rather malicious prank. Nasty, but not deadly."

"Mmmm," I murmured. Something was tickling inside my head. I was juggling the various bits of information we'd read about Gabbie Robinson on the Web. Judging a dog show ... dealing with cruelty cases ... and then there was that investigation that had been described as "ongoing".

Kyle's dog. A mastiff, with a tattered ear.

"What did you say mastiffs were bred for?"

"They were attack dogs," said Graham. "For use in battle. And in peacetime I think they were used for bear-baiting, dogfights, that kind of thing."

"Dogfighting! Gabbie was investigating something like that! And Kyle's dog has a ripped ear..." I stopped and looked at Graham. "What do you know about dogfights?"

Graham frowned. "Not a great deal," he confessed. "It was once socially acceptable but it's been illegal for years. People still do it, though. Some like it, strange as that seems. And there's a lot of money involved, what with the gambling and so on."

Kyle's face swam before my eyes. That nasty smirk when I'd asked about the packages ... yes, he seemed exactly the kind of person who would regard dogfights as light entertainment.

"You don't think Gabbie knew something about him, do you?" I said. "He looks the type to be involved in something really dodgy, don't you reckon?"

"It's perfectly possible," agreed Graham. "In fact, it seems quite likely to me. After all, we already know he has a criminal record. And if Gabbie knew something incriminating about him, it would have put her in a very dangerous position indeed."

fight club

The trouble was, we knew full well that Kyle Jacobs couldn't have killed Gabbie. We'd both seen him go into the shrubbery. But then he must have turned around, because he'd come back past us *before* Jessie had run off and Gabbie had gone in pursuit. Kyle Jacobs had been in full view when Gabbie was being bashed over the head.

"It was weird, though, him turning round," I said. "Why would he do that?"

"There could be a perfectly simple explanation. He could have changed his mind about where he wanted to walk."

"Or there could have been a reason for him wanting

to be in full view at the crucial moment…"

"What do you mean?"

"If he knew what was going to happen to her, he would have wanted to make sure no one suspected him," I said.

"So why did he go into the bushes in the first place?" asked Graham.

"I'm not sure." I considered the matter. "If he's involved with dodgy dogfights … well, it wouldn't be just him, would it? I mean, you couldn't do something like that on your own. There must be a whole gang of them."

"An accomplice," mused Graham. "Yes, that seems reasonable."

"And maybe Kyle was the only one who knew Gabbie by sight. Perhaps he pointed her out to the attacker. Someone who was already in the bushes, waiting for her."

My theory was taking shape nicely, so I ignored the odd feeling I'd had that Kyle had been telling the truth when he'd said he hadn't been in the shrubbery. I didn't want to be distracted from my train of thought. "So we're probably looking for a complete stranger…"

"The mysterious Mr X," said Graham. "Find him and the murder is solved."

We strolled on quietly while I thought back to the

evening of Gabbie's murder. It was strange that we hadn't noticed anyone, but then no one seemed to have seen anyone unusual. The police wouldn't have arrested Kathryn Hughes if there had been any other suspects, would they? And unfamiliar faces did get spotted: look at what had happened each time the film crew turned up. Poor Dermot O'Flannery had nearly been flattened by the crowd that had gathered to look at him.

Graham and I had slowly walked the three dogs all around the park and were coming back towards the side gate when we heard a peculiar noise coming from the shrubbery. It was halfway between a growl and a yelp, and for a moment I thought an animal was lurking in the undergrowth. Then I realized that whoever was making the sound was not only human, but suffering from some sort of Extreme Emotion. Sadness? Anger? It was difficult to tell. Graham and I looked at each other. As one we dropped to our hands and knees and crawled under the bushes so we could get closer. Intrigued, Bertie, Malcolm and Stanley followed.

From behind a large hydrangea we saw Grant Robinson kneeling on the ground exactly where his wife's body had been found. His arm was around Jessie, his face turned into her neck, and he was muttering into her fur. He had his back to us, so we couldn't see his expression. But we could hear what he was saying clearly enough.

"I don't understand," he was wailing miserably. "What went wrong?"

The dog licked him.

"It wasn't supposed to end like this!" he said angrily. "That was the whole point, wasn't it? No one else was supposed to get hurt! Nobody was supposed to get k—"

We would have heard a whole lot more if Bertie hadn't chosen that moment to break cover. He trundled out from under the bushes, closely followed by Malcolm and Stanley, and Jessie leapt up, eager to play. Grant stopped talking, stood up and glared at the little dogs. It was only then that I saw he hadn't been speaking to Jessie. He had a mobile in his hand, which he switched off before the person on the other end could reply. He looked dead guilty. For of course he knew that where there was a dog, an owner wouldn't be far behind.

We couldn't exactly pretend we hadn't been in the bushes. The only thing to do was make it look like we'd only just got there. I did a lot of rustling and then we both burst out, apparently out of breath.

"Have you seen Bertie?" I puffed, rushing across to Grant. "And the shih tzu? We've lost the lot!"

"Oh, there they all are!" exclaimed Graham, looking the picture of innocence. "Gosh! We were so worried.

What would we have said to their mummies?"

"Bertie's getting worse than Byron!" I realized as soon as the words slipped out that it wasn't the most tactful thing to have said, seeing as Byron was the one who had discovered Gabbie's body. A hot flush of embarrassment swept over me, but Grant didn't seem to notice – he was too busy trying to catch Jessie, who was bounding around with Malcolm and Stanley while Bertie looked on, a superior expression on his face.

Graham and I had no control whatsoever over the shih tzu, so it took a while for Grant to grab his dog and clip her on the lead. Once he'd managed it, he stalked off angrily, throwing a menacing look at me and Graham over his shoulder.

The encounter had left us with lots and lots to talk about. And the first thing I asked Graham was, what did he reckon Grant had been going to say before Bertie interrupted him? "Nobody was supposed to get killed"?

mr x

"**What** on earth is going on?" I plonked myself down on the spot where Gabbie Robinson had breathed her last. "Do you reckon Grant was talking about his wife's murder?"

"It's possible," said Graham, lowering himself onto a pile of dry leaves. "And if he was saying 'nobody was supposed to get *killed*', I think we can assume that the attacker was merely meant to rough her up a little."

"But what would be the point of that?" I asked, before answering my own question. "As a warning, maybe?"

Graham nodded. "Maybe. And if that was the case, it would seem to suggest that Gabbie knew too much.

Perhaps someone wanted to intimidate her to prevent her from finding out more about the dogfighting ring."

"But how come her husband's involved?" I asked. "It doesn't make sense." You only had to look at Grant with Jessie to see that he adored his dog – he was completely daft over her. A man who was that soppy couldn't possibly want to stand and watch dogs dying for his own amusement, could he? But, as that phone call had just proved, he certainly knew something.

"This is all getting too weird," I said. "If it *is* to do with dogfighting, Kyle's got to be involved. Grant clearly knows something about it. But neither of them can have killed Gabbie. Kathryn Hughes could have, but she's been in custody, so she can't have had anything to do with Mumsiewumsie's accident. The hit-and-run just has to be connected. But why would anyone want Mumsiewumsie dead? We're missing something, Graham. Come on, think."

I decided to start with Mumsiewumsie. All we knew about the car that had hit her was that it had a dog guard in it. So did Dermot's. But he'd said that he didn't keep a dog. He'd told us he didn't even like them.

Suppose he was lying?

My heart started to thump against my ribs. "Why would you lie about keeping a dog, Graham?"

"I have no idea," he said, looking at me closely. "I

suppose if you lived in a flat or somewhere you weren't allowed to keep pets."

"Weren't allowed?" I echoed. "Weren't allowed ... which would make it illegal. Like the dogfights. Dermot says he hasn't got a dog, but maybe he has. Maybe he just doesn't want to admit it because he's using it for something dodgy... It could have been him hiding in the bushes!"

"No, no, no," Graham said firmly. "The heat must be affecting your capacity for logical thought. Dermot O'Flannery cannot possibly be involved in this! He draws crowds like a magnet draws iron filings. If he'd been within a hundred metres of the park the day Gabbie Robinson was murdered, someone would have noticed. *We* would have noticed!"

Graham was right. Curse him. I deflated like a whoopee cushion. Sighing loudly, I tried again. Kyle Jacobs, I thought. What about him? I screwed my eyes tight shut and thought back over everything that had been said about him, hoping I might find a link to the mysterious Mr X – the stranger who'd lurked in the bushes. I turned over every last scrap of information and finally remembered what PC Black had said when we'd given him our statements right after Gabbie's murder. He'd let slip that Kyle "Horrible Hoodie" Jacobs was tagged. Minor theft, the policeman had said. So

Kyle hadn't been involved in anything serious. Or at least nothing that they knew about...

A flash of inspiration hit me like a thunderbolt. "Wasn't Dermot's house broken into the night his wife died?" I exclaimed.

"You know it was." Graham stayed annoyingly calm. "Her murder was the result of a bungled burglary."

"And Horrible Hoodie is tagged for theft."

"Minor theft." Graham shrugged. "They wouldn't let him walk the streets otherwise."

"Maybe he only got *caught* doing minor theft. It doesn't mean he's never done anything else."

"Are you suggesting he...?"

"Yes." I jumped to my feet, grabbing Graham's arm and pulling him up so forcefully that he squealed in protest.

We weren't any closer to finding Gabbie's killer. Or to knowing who'd driven the car that had knocked down Mumsiewumsie. But I was suddenly convinced that Horrible Hoodie had killed Dermot O'Flannery's wife.

"How? Why?" Graham puffed as we sped through the side gate of the park. I wanted to get as far away from there as possible.

"OK," I said as we raced along the pavement towards home. I'd picked Bertie up so we could move faster. Graham was dragging the doggy go-kart along with one hand and the two huffing, puffing shih tzu with the other. "I reckon they must have known each other from the dogfighting ring. I don't care what you say – Dermot's got a dog, I know he has. Maybe he uses it for fighting, I don't know. But he and Kyle are connected somehow, I'm sure of it. It's the only explanation. Dermot could have paid Kyle to kill his wife and make it look like a burglary."

"But why? He was devoted to her. He went to pieces! Fell into her grave and everything."

"Yes, well, Grant looks grief-stricken now too, doesn't he? And yet he spent all his time in the park flirting with Sprinting Woman before Gabbie died. Dermot's upset widower bit might just have been a good act. I bet his wife was well insured or something."

"Insurance money?" Graham nodded. "Yes, that sounds plausible. As we know, money is high on the list when it comes to murder motives."

"Exactly. And the case is still unsolved, which could be because up until now there's been nothing to connect Kyle and Dermot – nothing at all. Except for the dogfighting, which Gabbie Robinson, RSPCA inspector, was investigating. Suppose she was about to find out that they knew each other? Wouldn't that be enough for them to want to shut her up?"

"But where does Grant Robinson fit in? And Mumsie-wumsie?"

"I've no idea. But we'll work it out."

"So what do we do now?" asked Graham, sitting down on a wall and pausing to catch his breath.

"We've got no choice," I told him. "Let's call the police now. Tell them what we overheard, at any rate. Where's your phone?"

Graham plucked his mobile from his pocket but we were out of luck. After informing him that its battery was dangerously low, the mobile died with a soft, despairing bleep.

"Stupid thing!" I exclaimed crossly. I fought the urge to stamp on it. "We'll have to drop the dogs off and call from home, then."

Graham paled. "But your mum won't..."

"I'll distract her – you make the call."

Graham reluctantly agreed and we set off again. Cutting down a side street, we soon reached the alley that came out about a hundred metres from my house. We were only halfway down it, however, when a shadow fell across the exit. A man stood there, blocking our path.

The light was behind him and his hood was up. We couldn't see his face, but there was no mistaking the hellhound drooling on the end of its chain.

I'd talked to him earlier and he'd seemed OK. I told myself firmly that there was no reason to assume *he* knew that *we* knew about him. Kyle turning up right here, right now was just a harmless coincidence. I decided to ignore his threatening posture and attempt friendliness.

"Hi Kyle," I called hopefully. "OK, then?"

He didn't answer but squared his shoulders as if preparing for a fight. Then he murmured to his dog, and the beast started growling and straining impatiently, eager to attack. There was no doubt at all that he was on to us.

Graham and I froze. Malcolm and Stanley whimpered. Bertie barked, just once. We must have stood there for a good ten seconds, images of a painful death flashing through all of our heads, and then I had an idea.

"Back off," I whispered to Graham. "Nice and slow. We can get out the other way. He won't attack us when we're in the street. Too many witnesses."

Keeping our eyes firmly fixed on the slavering, snapping hellhound, we took a step back. Then another. We hadn't retreated more than three paces when we heard more growling, this time from behind us.

Unwilling to take my eyes off the killer dog in front of me, I snatched a quick glance over my shoulder.

"What on…?" I gasped. My heart plummeted into my shoes. A cold prickle of terror swept through me. Terror and confusion. Because Kyle was also standing behind us, hood up, hellhound snarling at the end of its chain.

"Graham," I said faintly, "there are two of them!"

Graham's jaw dropped. "What…? How…? I don't understand!" he squeaked.

But I did. Suddenly it all made sense. I wanted to kick myself for having been so stupid. All this time I'd been looking so hard for a connection, and yet there wasn't one.

That was the whole point.

"Horrible Hoodie was telling the truth!" I wailed. "I should have trusted my instincts. He must have come in through the side gate while we were watching Grant and Sprinting Woman. The guy we saw going into the bushes wasn't him! Same hoodie. Same breed of dog. Different man."

Graham looked from one advancing figure to the other and swallowed nervously. "So which of these is really Kyle Jacobs?"

"Neither of them," I said. "The police thought Mumsiewumsie was being absent-minded – that maybe she'd got the wrong day – but she wasn't. She saw Gabbie's murderer leaving through the back gate. That's why she got knocked down. They wanted her dead."

The dogs were closer now. Flecks of spittle hit the fences on either side of the alley. "Which one of you is Dermot?" I yelled.

For a second, both hounds and men stopped. The dogs strained at their leashes, but at a single command they both dropped to the ground. The man who had given it shook back his hood and smiled a charming Irish smile.

"Sure, you were right," he called to the second man. "They've worked it out. We should have been more careful."

"Let me guess." I turned to the other man and pointed an accusing finger. "You're Grant, right?"

Slowly, reluctantly, Grant Robinson peeled back his hood.

"No wonder Alexandra felt like you were using her," I said. "She must have come in very handy when you needed an alibi."

"Yeah, well…" Grant shuffled awkwardly from one foot to the other. At least he had the grace to look guilty.

Graham was working hard to catch up. "So where does Kyle fit in?" he asked.

"He doesn't," I said. "He's got nothing to do with any of it. Well, apart from maybe sending out those bags of dog poo. The first lot, anyway. I'll bet you did the second round, didn't you?"

Dermot smiled. "It helped muddy the waters," he said with a wink. "Confused the police a treat."

I was furious with myself. "Why didn't I see it before – it was so obvious!"

"What was?" demanded Graham.

"Two men *just happen* to lose their wives in tragic circumstances, and both of them are perfectly innocent because they *just happen* to have perfect alibis?" I glared at Dermot. "No wonder you didn't want to cover the poo package story. You didn't want any kind of link to be made between the two of you, did you? And if it hadn't been for Kyle's stupid little joke, no one would have known you two had ever met."

"But," said Graham, mystified, "I don't get it. Who's Mr X?"

"He is." I jerked my head towards Dermot. "It's true, isn't it? You killed Gabbie Robinson."

"Sure I did." Dermot sounded quite proud of himself. "You know, I couldn't see quite how to do it at first. Then I spotted that young lad. Distinctive hoodie? A mastiff just like mine? Perfect! The solution was so simple!"

"So that's why you lied about keeping dogs..." Graham looked thoughtful. "With the hood pulled over your face no one recognized you. We all assumed you were Kyle."

I looked from one man to the other. "You swapped murders, didn't you? You planned two killings committed by people so unconnected to their victims that the police would never solve them. You were total strangers, weren't you?"

"Strangers?" queried Graham. "Surely people don't hatch plans like this with people they don't even know?"

"Look at the way Alexandra was with Mum," I reminded him. "A bit of tea and sympathy and she was telling her whole life story." I turned back to Dermot. "So where did you first meet? On a train? In a pub?"

"In an airport lounge, actually." Dermot grinned. "The plane was delayed. We got talking. Found we had some problems in common. Wives: holding us back, getting in the way. Of course, I had the foresight to get mine well insured..."

"And you?" I glared at Grant. "Was Gabbie the same? Did you do it for the money, or what?"

"No!" protested Grant. "It wasn't that! I just didn't love her any more, that was all."

"Excuse me," said Graham politely, "but if that was the case, wouldn't a simpler solution have been to divorce her?"

A dark cloud of fury suddenly contorted Grant's handsome surfer-boy features. "She would have taken Jessie away from me."

A tug of love over a golden retriever? It seemed so ridiculous I almost laughed out loud. But hey, we were in a parallel universe. Somehow, on Planet Dog, murdering someone over a canine figured.

"Hang on, though," Graham objected. "I thought we'd decided Gabbie wasn't supposed to get killed. When Grant was on the phone, didn't he say...?"

"No," I interrupted with a tired sigh. "I was wrong about that, too. He wasn't talking about Gabbie. He was talking about Kathryn Hughes. A young mum arrested. Two small kids at home." I eyed Grant. "You felt bad about it, didn't you? That was what you were about to say. It wasn't 'nobody was supposed to get *killed*'; it was 'nobody was supposed to get *caught*'. You felt guilty about her being charged."

"It was a good plan!" cried Grant. "Flawless. No one else was supposed to get hurt." He looked at Dermot accusingly. "No one was supposed to get arrested!"

I detected friction between the conspirators. If we could use it, we had a slim chance of survival.

Dermot broke in on the conversation. "There's nothing we can do to help Kathryn," he said. "She'll be convicted. The Braithwaite woman will die – I'll see to that. And you two... Innocent kids killed by strays? Urban dogs are such a menace! You know, I might just do a feature on it. Let's get on, shall we?"

We'd been standing in the alleyway chatting like dog walkers on a Sunday afternoon. But now Dermot bent down to the hellhound at his side and slipped the chain over its head.

I swung around to face Grant. "Are you going to let him do this?"

Grant winced. In a voice husky with emotion he said, "We can't let you go. I can't end up in prison. Who'd look after Jessie?" He slipped the other dog off its chain.

Death came a heartbeat closer.

But if I'd learned one thing during all those strolls in the park it was that dog owners like to talk about their pets. Frantically I asked Dermot, "What's his name?"

"Bruno," replied Dermot smoothly. "And behind you is Frazier."

"Oh?" Graham chipped in helpfully. "They're both yours, are they?"

"They are."

"Did you use the clicker method?" asked Graham. "Only, they seem far better trained than Kyle's dog."

"Oh, they are." Dermot smiled. "They're trained to attack." He grinned another cheeky grin. And then calmly, clearly, he commanded his dogs: "Kill."

Bruno and Frazier leapt forward. The shih tzu fled, yelping.

A gust of hot, flesh-eating breath. A flash of tearing teeth. Blood-chilling snarls. I couldn't help it – I dropped Bertie and grabbed Graham. There was nowhere to run and nowhere to hide. All we could do was shut our eyes, hide our faces in each other's shoulders and wait to be torn apart. It wasn't going to be quick and it wasn't going to be painless. Frankly, I whimpered. We both did. I've never been so scared in my life.

But I hadn't reckoned on Bertie.

The King of Charisma was None Too Pleased about being dropped, but luckily for us his deep suspicion of Graham and me was a thing of the past. He'd decided that we were his Personal Property. Nothing and no one was allowed near what Bertie considered rightfully his.

He pulled his Oriental lips back into a contemptuous sneer. Then he growled.

The mastiffs literally turned in mid-air. As they crashed to the ground you could almost see the puzzled doggy thought bubbles pop out of their heads. Bertie growled again.

It wasn't what you'd call impressive. He was a fraction of their size and there were two of them. They could have swallowed Bertie in one gulp. But the supreme self-confidence gleaming in his bulgy eyes together with his total lack of fear had an astonishing effect. Both killer dogs suddenly clamped their tails between their legs, took a step back and let out a confused whine.

"Kill!" This time Dermot's command was neither calm nor clear. It was panicked. The dogs didn't move. "Kill! For God's sake, kill them!" He was getting desperate. The TV reporter waved his arms, flapping them up and down furiously and making his dogs even more anxious and confused. Clearly he hadn't read Graham's *Complete Dog Maintenance Manual*. The more he yelled and flapped, the less control he had over his dogs.

Bertie stood looking calmly from one dog to the other. Grant seemed about to burst into tears but Dermot was incensed. He'd killed Gabbie without any qualms. He'd knocked down Mumsiewumsie without a second thought. Disposing of two children should have been all in a day's work. And if the dogs weren't going to do it, he would.

When the charming Irish reporter came for us, all we had to defend ourselves with was the doggy go-kart. It was no use as an escape vehicle, but as a weapon it proved surprisingly effective.

As Dermot lunged, Graham smashed the skateboard into his head, leaving a gaping wound.

Maybe it was the smell of blood. Maybe the dogs were wound up by Dermot's frenzied commands. But when he reeled backwards and trod on Bruno's paw, Bruno yelped and snapped at him. His teeth connected with the reporter's hand and he screamed. Frazier – not wanting to miss out on doing what he'd been trained for – sprang at him. Graham and I were knocked aside. Dermot's shriek of alarm was cut short. And suddenly there was an awful lot of blood.

Grant turned and ran. Big mistake. The mastiffs threw back their heads and bayed, then gave chase. Tongues lolling out, the dogs bounded past us. Grant was brought down before he'd even reached the street.

Right in front of our eyes, both men had their throats torn out like ancient Aztec warriors.

There's not much to add, really. Dermot and Grant died of their injuries and sadly the mastiffs had to be put down: the RSPCA said that once they had developed a taste for blood, they couldn't be trusted not to attack again.

Mumsiewumsie recovered from her accident and was soon back walking Malcolm and Stanley twice a day in the park. Jessie was rehomed and ended up living with the Ball Obsessed Collie. Kathryn Hughes was released without charge.

No one ever did get prosecuted for sending out the poo packages. I was pretty sure Horrible Hoodie had done it, but I wasn't going to say anything. You see, Graham and I became quite friendly with Kyle Jacobs in the end. He still looked scary – and so did his dog – but we discovered that they really were both as soft as butter underneath. And Kyle had been telling the truth about Tyson's ear – it had been ripped in a fight, but there was nothing illegal about it. Gertrude the dachshund had bitten him and Tyson hadn't even retaliated. As for Kyle's criminal record and the theft he'd been tagged for, it turned out that he'd nicked some doggy treats from the local pet shop. Not entirely honest, maybe, but not exactly a Major Crime, either.

Graham and I carried on walking Bertie until Mrs Biggs's leg healed, which wasn't until a few weeks into the new school year. By then, I'd become quite attached to him. Well, you can't help liking an animal that's saved your life, can you? Even if it does look like a hairy maggot.

1

Has the past come back to haunt them?

My name is Poppy Fields. I never believed in ghosts – until I stayed on a remote Scottish island, and people started dropping dead all over the place. Was a spirit taking revenge? When Graham and I investigated, we began to see right through it...

mondays are murder

zombies?
spooks?
or just plain murder?

tanya landman

2

That's the way to do it!

My name is Poppy Fields. I was dead excited about my first trip to America. But then people started getting themselves killed in really weird ways. Nothing made sense until Graham and I investigated, then the murders seemed to tie together as neatly as a string of sausages. A little *too* neatly...

dead funny

can you die laughing?

tanya landman

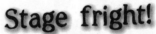

Stage fright!

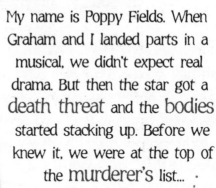

My name is Poppy Fields. When Graham and I landed parts in a musical, we didn't expect real drama. But then the star got a death threat and the bodies started stacking up. Before we knew it, we were at the top of the murderer's list...

On the trail of a murderer!

My name is Poppy Fields. When we designed a murder mystery trail for the school fayre, it was supposed to be a bit of fun. But before long the head was dead and Graham and I were hunting down a real life killer.

Murder is a beastly business!

My name is Poppy Fields. Graham and I were first on the scene at a series of murders at the zoo, but who was behind them? We had to prowl around a bit to investigate – and what we saw was not pretty. How would we escape before we, too, became dead meat?

Roll up, roll up!

My name is Poppy Fields. When the circus came to town, the posters promised certain death. This made Graham and me suspicious, and we were proved right when someone was killed in the ring. With the circus performers still in grave danger, we had to work fast to discover who was firing the shots...

7

Words can be dangerous.

My name is Poppy Fields. When we offered to help out at our local literary festival, Graham and I had no idea just how murky the world of children's books really was. Before you could say crime novel, the authors were receiving anonymous threats. Then fiction started turning into fact...

Greek tragedy?

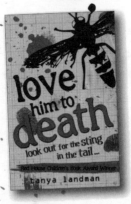

My name is Poppy Fields. When Graham and I jetted off to the celebrity wedding of the century, I couldn't believe my luck. Sun, sea, scandal – what more could anyone wish for? But then things turned nasty, and when people started dropping like flies it was time to investigate...